ISBN 978-1-332-85208-6
PIBN 10222324

1 MONTH OF
FREE
READING

at
www.ForgottenBooks.com

By purchasing this book you are eligible for one month membership to ForgottenBooks.com, giving you unlimited access to our entire collection of over 700,000 titles via our web site and mobile apps.

To claim your free month visit:
www.forgottenbooks.com/free222324

English
Français
Deutsche
Italiano
Español
Português

www.forgottenbooks.com

Mythology Photography **Fiction**
Fishing Christianity **Art** Cooking
Essays Buddhism Freemasonry
Medicine **Biology** Music **Ancient
Egypt** Evolution Carpentry Physics
Dance Geology **Mathematics** Fitness
Shakespeare **Folklore** Yoga Marketing
Confidence Immortality Biographies
Poetry **Psychology** Witchcraft
Electronics Chemistry History **Law**
Accounting **Philosophy** Anthropology
Alchemy Drama Quantum Mechanics
Atheism Sexual Health **Ancient History**
Entrepreneurship Languages Sport
Paleontology Needlework Islam
Metaphysics Investment Archaeology
Parenting Statistics Criminology
Motivational

THE LINK

Program Magazine for the
United Fellowship of Protestan¹

STAFF

EDITOR: Joe Dana; EDITORIAL SECRETARY: Kay Powell; CIRCULA
TION MANAGER: Isabel R. Senar.   PUBLISHER: Marion J. Creeg·

Member of The Associated Church Press

Bible quotations are from the Revised Standard Version unless otherwise note·

Subscription prices to civilians: $2.00 a year; $1.50 a year in lots of ten or more to one address

For chaplains: Bulk orders to bases for free distribution to personnel are invoiced quarterly at the rate of 10c per copy. Special options are open to chaplains whose funds do not allow payment of this cost.

Published monthly by The General Commission on Chaplains and Armed Forces Personnel at 815 Demonbreun St., Nashville 3, Tenn. Entered as second-class matter at the Post Office, Nashville, Tenn., under the Act of March 3, 1879.

Address all correspondence to the Editor at 122 Maryland Ave., NE., Washington 2, D.C.

Christmas Lambs

by Herbert Witten

THE WHITLOWS arose early Christmas morning. When Tad and Jamie found all the toys a child could ask for under the tree, they shouted and bounced in glee. Fletch Whitlow and his wife, Bess, and their parents, who had come to spend Christmas with them, filled to overflowing with pride. They laughed as the children discovered each toy.

Soon Tad, with the aid of his grandparents, had the tracks laid for his electric train, and it went careening around the rails. There were tricycles, trucks, cars, airplanes, and many other things. Jamie had two or three big life-like dolls, a doll house with furniture and dishes, and a dozen other nice presents.

Fletch hurriedly gulped a cup of coffee and donned his heavy clothes before going down to the big barn to do his feeding. His hired hand had decided to take the week off right when Fletch needed him most.

"Hope those sheep have come in this morning," Fletch said.

"They probably came in during the night," Bess said.

"It's about time for some of the ewes to lamb," Fletch said as he got up and put his cap on. "They're awfully early this year."

He stepped outside. It was just breaking day. A heavy snow blanketed the ground, and it was still snowing. Huge flakes floated softly downward through the still air.

He was just kindhearted and was forever letting people trample on him.

Fletch remembered the old foreigner and his family who moved in a week or two ago. The old man had asked Fletch for work. He was thin and stooped, his pale face as narrow as an axe blade. His eyes were big and mild.

"I just take any kind of work," the old man, who earlier told Fletch his name was Remstedt, said in a soft voice. "I'm not so strong, but I do my best."

"Naw, naw, I haven't got anything for you to do," Fletch said tartly. "Keep off my property."

Mr. Remstedt ducked his head. "I mean no harm to you," he said meekly. "We have much sickness, my family hungry." He paused and stared at his hands. "It'll soon be Christmas."

"I'm sorry, old man," Fletch said brusquely. "You'll have to work like other folks. I haven't anything to give you."

used keen judgment, and had prospered.

He went hurriedly across his broad fields. They lay white and smooth all around him, and gently rolled and swelled in the distance. There wasn't a blemish on them anywhere. There were no gullies or bushes; the meadows and pastures were smooth. Last year's cornfields were in heavy cover crops.

The orchards, stretched endlessly on the upper end of the vast farm, were exceptionally beautiful under their robes of snow.

Fletch hastened his steps as he fanned the smoldering dislike for the foreigners to hot anger. They probably broke a wire on his fence, or left the upper gate open and let his sheep get out.

The snow was sticky and slippery under his feet. He kept looking all around, but he saw no sign of the sheep. No doubt about it, they were out. He gave up finding them in the pasture and headed straight for the upper gate.

Just as he figured, it was standing wide open. He swept through it, his anger boiling.

THE WIND HAD BEEN BLOWING yesterday before it started snowing, but Fletch was sure that it hadn't blown the gate open. Those foreigners had left it open. He hurried to their cabin in the little hollow beyond his pasture.

It was a drab, unsightly looking place. The house was made of rough lumber, with wide cracks where the boards had warped and sprung. The windows were broken and covered with cardboard boxes. A thin wisp of smoke hung in the air above the house.

A dog barked when Fletch approached. It was full daylight now. Fletch noticed the sagging log barn across the hollow from the house. He paused at the rock in front of the porch which served as steps. Then he stepped up on the low, rotten porch. He walked cautiously on the boards for fear they would give way with him. Just as he reached to rap on the door he heard someone call.

"Mister Whitlow."

Mr. Remstedt had come out of the barn and motioned for Fletch, "Down here."

Fletch retraced his steps back off the porch. Now what does he want, he thought irritably. He followed the well-beaten path through the snow, wondering why they had made so many trips to the barn this early in the morning.

The old man waited in front of the barn. Fletch eyed him questioningly.

"What do you want?"

"Come inside the barn." He turned and walked through the door.

"I'm looking for some lost sheep," Fletch said gruffly. "Have you seen any sign of 'em?"

Mr. Remstedt led him to the back of the barn without replying. He held a stall door open for Fletch, who hesitated, then stepped inside. He stopped with a gasp of amazement. In the big stall that ran the entire width of the barn were at least twenty head of his prize ewes. It looked as if each one had a lamb.

"They come to my place about midnight," Mr. Remstedt explained, "Eric there, he hear them; go outside and find." He nodded at a tousled-haired, sharp-faced youth of about fifteen, who was working efficiently with the ewes and lambs.

3

"We've been working with them all night."

Fletch kept his eyes on the floor of the stall. Without looking directly at either the old man or his son, he stole a glance around the stall. Fodder had been strewn on the floor, and bundles of it had been stacked around the walls to keep out the cold. Old sacks and rags that they had used to rub dry the newborn lambs lay in a manger.

Mr. Remstedt kept looking at Fletch as though he sought approval for the kind deed they had done. Suddenly he grinned broadly, "I almost forget, there's one more up at the house. He very weak, we think him die if he no get warm. His mama, she not let him nurse."

Eric picked up a kinky-haired lamb and stroked it gently. He kept his eyes on Fletch.

"My children like lamb. They pet nearly all night." His voice grew low. "We have no money to buy things for Christmas. They get joy out of little, tiny lamb."

"Leif wanted a train," Eric said sullenly, his piercing blue eyes on Fletch. "He's very sick, maybe die. He wanted a train for Christmas. But he not get. Father not get job to buy food, much less train. Leif die."

"Eric!" Mr. Remstedt said sharply.

The boy continued to stroke the lamb. Fletch shifted uneasily. He pretended to stare at a ewe and a lamb in a far corner, but he didn't see them. His mind was filled with troubled, self-condemning thoughts. He remembered this pathetic man almost begging him for work, and he had very coldly turned a deaf ear. He heard himself again, speaking sharply, rudely to him, ordering him off his place.

4

Now the old man through gentle kindness had tossed it right back in his face. They had taken care of his ewes and lambs, and watched them through the long night, keeping them warm and safe from the wind and snow. No doubt all the lambs would otherwise have died as soon as they were born.

"Come up to house," Mr. Remstedt said. "See lamb. Children not want to let it go."

Reluctantly Fletch followed. He glanced back as he stepped through the stall door. Eric's dark eyes were on him; his lips were a thin, grim line.

Fletch followed the man through the deep snow to the house. He noticed the narrow shoulders, slightly bent, but the step was springy. It was then Fletch realized that Mr. Remstedt wasn't as old as he appeared. He was more undernourished than anything else.

They reached the house. Mr. Remstedt very politely opened the door and told Fletch to enter. Fletch stepped inside.

THERE WAS A WOMAN SITTING BEfore the fire in a straight-back chair. She had a shawl thrown over her narrow shoulders. They had a cot pulled up close to the fire, and a little boy about the age of Tad lay on it, playing with the lamb. Two more children younger than he crowded close. When they saw Fletch, they sidled around to the far side of the cot and eyed him shyly. The little boy on the cot was pale and sickly looking. He stared at Fletch out of eyes much too big for his birdlike face.

Fletch knew this was Leif, the one Eric had mentioned.

The woman nodded and smiled tiredly when her husband introduced them. Fletch took in the room. It was nearly bare. There were two iron bedsteads, the cot the boy lay on, a dresser, three chairs, and a nailkeg, used for a chair.

There were cracks in the floor big enough to put his fingers through. A small fire flickered on the hearth. Fletch noticed that, though the place was meagerly furnished and drafty, it was clean as a pin. The walls had been papered with newspapers. The bedclothes were faded and tattered, but clean.

"Sit down," said Mr. Remstedt.

"No, thanks," Fletch mumbled.

"Look how strong the lamb is now," Mr. Remstedt said proudly.

Fletch nodded.

"You're not going to take it?" the boy cried, and pulled it close to him. "It's mine. It's my Christmas present."

"It belongs to Mister Whitlow," the man said.

The boy stared wide-eyed at Fletch, and pulled farther back. "The lamb's mine. I wanted a train for Christmas, but I didn't get it. I got the lamb."

"The boy is very sick; the doctors say if he not get good treatment, he may—may—" his voice trailed off.

Suddenly Fletch shook himself out of the trance he'd been in for the last few minutes.

"I'll not take your lamb, son. You can keep him."

"Thank you, sir," the little boy said, stroking the lamb. Tears trickled down his pale cheeks.

Fletch turned and walked to the door, Mr. Remstedt followed. When they were outside, Fletch said, "Come along with me. I'll take you down to the store and pay you for taking care of the sheep."

"No, no," Mr. Remstedt shook his head vigorously. "You owe me nothin'."

"I want to pay you," Fletch said. "Come along now."

"No, no," Mr. Remstedt repeated. "I not like to see animals suffer, and I do my neighbor favor."

Fletch smiled sheepishly, "I want to do my neighbor a favor, too; so I'm going to pay you."

"But I not want take anything. Anyway the store will be closed to-day. It's Christmas."

"I got a friend that sells general merchandise," Fletch told him. "He sells groceries, toys, clothes, almost anything you can think of. I reckon he's even got a train or two laying around."

"You very kind, Mister Whitlow," he brushed his eyes with his coat sleeve.

"A man should treat his neighbors and workhands well," Fletch said as he turned and led the way down through his pasture. "You and your oldest boy can start working for me Monday."

"Thank you, and God bless you," the man whispered softly.

"Let me thank you," Fletch said. "And I don't mean for taking care of my lost sheep."

The man looked at him curiously for a moment, then looked away, making no comment—as though he understood.

When they passed through the pasture gate, Fletch pulled it closed to fasten the latch. He stood there for a moment staring at the catch. It was broken! It was then he remembered bumping it with his hay baler a few weeks before.

WHENCE THE CHRISTMAS CARD?

By VINCENT EDWARDS

WHAT PERSON is there who does not feel a certain tingle of excitement as Uncle Sam's letter carriers make their rounds at this time of year? Practically everybody is looking forward to what these busy couriers will leave at his door. There are bundles and packages, but by far the larger part of the postman's back-breaking load is composed of the familiar yuletide greeting cards.

Those stacks of square white envelopes with their gay seals fairly shout of holiday good cheer. As we run through the heart-warming messages, coming from old friends who have not been seen for long months, we can almost hear the festive chimes of the season ringing in the distance. Such is the spell cast by the Christmas card of our day.

Curiously enough, the custom of sending such greetings does not date back much more than a century. It was one hundred and eleven years ago this Christmas that the idea was first put into practice.

It all started in 1845 because a busy Englishman found that he would not have time to write the letters he usually sent off to friends in the holiday season. Sir Henry Cole's days were so crowded that he simply could not squeeze in all that extra correspondence. It seemed, at first, as if his relatives and friends were due for a disappointment.

Then he had an inspiration. Sir Henry engaged a promising young artist, John Calcott Horsley, to design a card that could be sent out to all the persons he usually remembered.

The greeting that Horsley made was strikingly artistic and quite like the cards of today. It was rectangular in shape, decorated with a leafy trellis work. It was divided into three panels, two small ones and a large one in the center.

The smaller panels pictured acts of charity—"feeding the hungry" on one and "clothing the naked" on the other. In the larger one was pictured a happy family group of three generations. At the top right corner was the word "To ——" with space for the receiver's name. In the bottom right corner was a similar arrangement of "From ——" for the name of the sender.

After John Horsley had completed his design, copies were made by a printer. They were then colored by hand. One thousand copies were finished for Sir Henry Cole.

The unusual form of greeting

made a great hit with all his friends. It is this card, copies of which are still to be seen in England today, that is regarded as the forerunner of the modern commercial Christmas card.

Not long afterward a London artist, Joseph Cundall, put the idea into commercial use. He became the first Christmas card publisher. The first season he designed only one card. It turned out that only a few hundred were sold, but the public was beginning to get the habit.

Then came the 1860's, and people almost tumbled over one another, trying to buy Christmas greeting cards. Young people of those days never forgot the thrill of getting their first cards in the mail. The custom had not become as universal as it has in our time, but hundreds of cards were purchased. Some of these had very crude drawings—a snow-covered church with a spray of holly wreathing it, or a chill, wintry road along which walked a bent old man under a heavy burden of faggots.

America's first important Christmas card publisher was Louis Prang. Prang was a political refugee from the Germany of Bismarck. Fleeing to this country after the revolution of 1848, he turned to good account his knowledge of lithography. At Roxbury, Massachusetts, he founded the firm of L. Prang and Company.

It was not until 1874 that the company started printing Christmas cards on a large scale. The cards made an instant hit with the American public, and became so celebrated that Mr. Prang even received many orders from England.

In those days, when a young lady was remembered with one of these cards at Christmas, she often told in her diary of the "beautiful Prang" she had received. In publishing his cards, Mr. Prang brought to perfection a lithographic process which sometimes used as many as twenty colors.

It was in the 1880's that Christmas cards became real works of art. The reason was obvious—not until then did publishers start paying big prices to artists. Famous painters pricked up their ears when the great firm of Raphael Tuck and Sons announced its offer of five hundred guineas in prizes—over $2,500—for the best designs. In the exciting contest that followed, some of Great Britain's leading artists had their work accepted. Among them were Sir John Millais, Marcus Stone, George Boughton, and James Sant.

In America, similar contests took place, and Louis Prang's company was the leader in trying to interest artists. Hundreds of designs were submitted, and judges often had quite a time trying to choose the winners. When a painter won out, he always found the award worth while. In one of Mr. Prang's spirited competitions, a girl artist, Dora Wheeler, once walked away with two thousand dollars.

Today, Christmas cards are more the rage than ever. There has been a marked improvement in printing in recent years, with the high-speed presses that have been developed. The famous firm of Raphael Tuck still offers its attractive work, while, in America, holiday cards have become so artistic that the Metropolitan Museum of New York now selects a number of subjects from its galleries for reproduction.

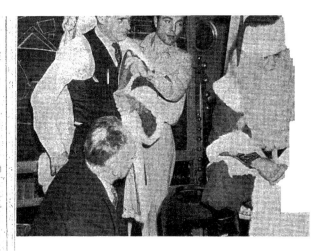

Trainer
For Santa Claus

Josephine M. Opsahl

CHARLES HOWARD has one of the most glamorous jobs in the world. He is not only America's best-loved Santa Claus, but his school at Albion, New York, known as Santa Claus College, is the only one of its kind in the world.

The schoolhouse for this unusual institution is Howard's own home, a large colonial country house about a century and a quarter old. Santa Claus College is set far back from the highway on a spacious shaded lawn. Filled with antiques and traditions, it breathes the spirit of Christmas.

Unlike most schools, Santa Claus College operates for only a short time each year. There are two or three terms, beginning the last week of October. Enrollment is limited to fifteen pupils a term. Classes are from 9:00 A.M. through 4:30 in the afternoon. They start on Monday morning, with graduation Friday evening. If necessary, Saturday is used for review and for finishing work. After one year's successful work, the coveted degree of "Bachelor of Santa Claus" is given to all graduates.

Charles Howard has had a keen interest in childhood's beloved saint for many years. When he was a

8

chubby fourth-grader, his mother made him a Santa suit so that he could play the part at a school program. For many years following he was asked to be Santa whenever one was needed in the community.

This interest in Santa also grows out of his work. In addition to operating a fair-sized farm, Howard makes toys to sell in nearby cities. While delivering his toys, he studied the department store's Santas closely. He found that most of them poorly portrayed the gentle old saint. Their clothing was shoddy and neglected. Their actions often frightened little children. Many did not even fulfill their purpose of helping the stores to sell toys.

Mr. Howard studied all angles of the Santa problem. He felt that small children regarded Santa as extra special, and that they approached him with a mingled feeling of love and fear. He claimed that Santa represented the spirit of Christmas and should be more than a jovial clown seated on a throne. In fact, to be really effective at this busiest of seasons, Santa should be working in his toyshop. This would make children lose their shyness and help Santa to aid their parents in selecting the right toys.

About twenty years ago, Howard had a chance to put his theories into practice at a large Rochester, New York, department store. While he had looked forward to this work under almost ideal conditions, he had so many problems and trials the first day that he dreaded the weeks to follow. The second morning, however, he noticed a little girl in the crowd. Her eyes were wide with worship and wonder. Finally, approaching him, she timidly asked

if she could touch his beard. Patting it lovingly, she asked, "Santa, will you promise me something?"

Although Howard, as Santa, is usually reticent about making promises, he did this time.

"Will you promise, Santa," she asked, "never to cut your whiskers?"

Howard said that her love for Santa revealed to him the need of really being Santa. During the following weeks, consequently, he worked and talked as "Santa." This new type of Santa drew such crowds that the following year he had many requests for his services.

As he was thinking about his inability to be in several places at one time, he discussed with a friend the possibility of setting up a school to train others. The friend, a newspaperman, asked permission to use the idea for a story. As a result, Howard received many applications to attend the proposed school.

He selected the members of his first class carefully. Of the six he chose, two were women. One wanted to study for the role of Mrs. Santa, and the other as Santa's secretary.

9

After being called together by the ringing of sleigh bells, the first class opened with the singing of Jingle Bells. Prayer was offered by a local clergyman. Then followed an intensive week of study and discussion. Interviewing a group of school children, these first student Santas learned ideas about Santa which are not found in books. They also talked to members of all the local Parent-Teacher Associations, to department store heads, and to toymakers. They discussed Santa's personal appearance. They talked about what they should know regarding Santa Claus stories, legends, and songs.

This first class was held in 1937. Through the years, the course of study has been added to and revised many times.

In order to graduate, Howard's pupils must learn all about the origin, history, and showmanship of the jolly old saint whom they are emulating, as well as all the well-known Christmas stories, songs, and

10

legends. They must also learn the art of make-up, the choice and care of their costumes, and the most efficient settings for Santa Claus. They study what the customer, the store, and the child expect of Santa, child psychology, and proper toys for children of all ages and their educational value. They practice Christmas decorations, wrappings, games for parties. The session known as the "laughing class" is one of the noisiest and merriest of all. Here all Santas practice laughing in a deep-seated, jolly way.

To complete this intensive course of work, Howard's pupils have a practice lesson at one of the local schools. All Albion school children know that Howard is a good friend of Santa's. They are not surprised to have him, accompanied by the good Christmas saint, visit their classroom.

Santa's classmates, not in costume, sit in the back of the room and watch the student act his part. When they are all back in their own classroom, they discuss his performance and suggest ways for that Santa to better his technique.

Howard does not train Santas and rent them out to department stores. There has been so much demand for all his Santas that today many department stores are sending their own personnel to be trained for the job. Up to this time, approximately 500 Santas have graduated from Santa Claus College.

Anyone can tell the difference between a rightly-trained Santa and the regular run. Even children notice the difference. One small child was heard telling his parents, "Let's not see any more Santas. I think this is the real one."

RECONVERSION

By
Ruth Mundorff

"Hi, Tom!"

"Huh?" Sgt. Tom Lawrence looked up through the driving rain and recognized a friend. "Oh hi, Bill," he replied without enthusiasm, almost resenting his friend's cheerful smile.

"You don't look happy," Bill said, as they walked together toward the bus stop at Tachikawa Air Base, near Tokyo, Japan.

"That's putting it mildly," agreed Tom, who at this moment looked every inch the tough sergeant. His mouth was pulled down at one corner. His gray eyes appeared cold and unfriendly as they squinted against the rain. In his right hand he clenched a book with unnecessary intensity, as if it were a Tommy gun.

"Come on, now," said Bill, " 'Christmas comes but once . . . '"

"Finish that quotation and I'll brain you," said Tom.

Silently they climbed onto the Air Force bus and found a couple of seats together near the rear.

Some people just cannot keep quiet for any length of time, and Bill was such a man. "What's eating you?" he asked his friend after they had traveled a few blocks over the bumpy road. "And how come you're going into Tokyo? I thought your squadron was throwing a big shindig tonight back in Tachi."

"Yeah," said Tom. "And I've gotta miss it, all on account of I was a fool." Tom explained that in a susceptible moment he had agreed to teach an English conversation class at a Japanese business college one night a week.

Ordinarily he didn't mind, even almost enjoyed it. It was good for laughs. The students, although they were about his own age, made him feel like a *honcho*. But he sure hated missing the squadron party, and having to spend Christmas Eve trying to teach English grammar.

"I shoulda just sent word I was sick," Tom finished. "I wish I had now." To change the subject, he asked, "Where're you headed?"

"I thought I'd go to the USO," Bill answered, "and then take in the 2300 candlelight service at the chapel center. What time do you finish your class?"

"Ten-thirty."

11

"Then how about meeting me at the chapel?"

"No, count me out. I'll be too tired after teaching for two hours and a half. Besides, I—to put it frankly—I don't feel like Christmas this year. You get a long ways away from home and out of the habit of going to church. You mail your Christmas presents in October. Well, Christmas is just one more day in the week."

"I'm sorry you feel that way," said Bill, dropping the subject.

Sgt. Lawrence's resentment was still with him when he started his class. The schoolroom was poorly lighted. A crude wood stove failed to have much effect on the chilly, wet air. Instead of the bantering he usually started with to warm up the class psychologically, this evening he began immediately with the lesson. He opened his book, which was entitled *Teaching English as a Foreign Language*.

"Today we will talk about the proper use of the verb 'do' as an auxiliary," he said. "All of you need to learn this. You all make mistakes because you don't know this verb."

The class looked disappointed and cowed, but Sgt. Lawrence went doggedly on with his exposition. Almost deliberately he used words like "periphrastic" which the class could not be expected to understand. After fifteen minutes of this two students went to sleep. Others looked bored or puzzled.

"What's the matter with this class tonight?" demanded Sgt. Lawrence in exasperation, thinking about the party he was missing back at the base. "Don't you want to learn the English language? What are you taking this class for?"

ONE TADEO KUMATA SPOKE UP timidly. "We were hoping you are telling us tonight about Christmas."

Sgt. Lawrence looked at the serious expressions on the fifty non-Christian faces in front of him and suddenly laughed. With that, he relaxed into more like his usual good fellowship, and closed his book. "You win," he said. "What do you want to know about Christmas?"

"We are wanting to know everything about it," said Mr. Kumata.

liked a little time to think through how to present this subject.

But one of the students answered, "It is birthday of Jesus. It is from birthday of Jesus the Christians are starting the calendars."

"Fine. Jesus was born about 1956 years ago. Does anybody know where?"

"Bellingham?" suggested one student after a considerable pause.

"Almost," laughed the teacher. "Jesus was born in Bethlehem. Where is that?"

"Pennsylvania," came an answer.

At this point, mercifully, the bell rang for a ten-minute break. Sgt. Lawrence went into the office and gratefully accepted a cup of tea from the secretary. He still had over an hour of class time and pondered how best to tell the Japanese students about Christmas. He looked in his textbook but found nothing on the subject.

With five minutes of recess remaining, he struck upon an excellent idea and acted upon it. He would pray for divine guidance. God ought to be as interested as Sgt. Lawrence in how Christmas was discussed.

"Lord," he prayed, "please help me out with this class tonight. They want to know about Christmas. You know I'm no missionary, or even one of your better servants. But I'd like to give them as clear and true a picture as possible."

He went back into the class with more confidence. "Are you Christian?" asked one of the students before Sgt. Lawrence could get started.

"Yes," the sergeant answered, "I am." There was no reason to confuse the students with any of his backslidings. "And, as a Christian, this is what I believe."

He told then in very simple language about how the ancient Jews had looked for a Messiah, about the annunciation to Mary, and the birth in a manger. As he did so, the whole beautiful story came to him with a new freshness and excitement. He was further exhilarated by the keen interest on the part of his listeners.

"Why wasn't God making a room in the inn?" asked one.

"Maybe he wanted to teach us to adapt ourselves to hardships. Jesus never tried to make things easy for himself. He showed how a man could lead a perfect life in spite of troubles and disappointments." Sgt. Lawrence thought guiltily of his own disappointment in missing the party and with what bad grace he had taken it.

"Are all Americans Christian?" asked Mr. Kumata.

"Not quite," Sgt. Lawrence answered. "And none of us are perfect Christians like Jesus. But our laws and our ideals are based on Christianity. So if you want to understand Americans, it helps to understand Christianity."

The closing bell rang while the class still had questions. Sgt. Lawrence answered as many as he could, and told the more eager students where they could find missionaries who would tell them more.

A few minutes later, Sgt. Lawrence again ran into his friend. "I thought you weren't coming," said Bill, as they met in front of the chapel. The rain was still pouring down, but the strains of "Adeste Fidelis" burst from the church.

"I changed my mind," said Lawrence. It's a funny thing. But even 2,000 miles from home, Christmas can be exciting after all."

SANTA WAS A THIN MAN

Louise Berthold

WOULD it surprise you to learn that until the early 1900's children of many countries pictured Santa as a tall, thin, anemic-looking old gentleman with doleful eyes and a mouth that turned down at the corners? Indeed, he was so skinny that he looked as if he had resisted firmly the temptation to sample even one of the millions of goodies he prepared each year for well-behaved children all over the world.

Instead of the picturesque, comfortable costume he wears today, he was then dressed in a short, close-fitting, ermine-trimmed coat and long tights that gave him the appearance of a jester in the court of King Charles. His only resemblance to our modern, roly-poly, merry-eyed Santa was his long white beard.

But if his physical appearance lacked color, his speech did not. On a Christmas card issued in the year of 1882 he bombastically wished for people everywhere "A Most Consummate Xmas & An Utterly Utter

● The Santa pictured here still has Saint Nicholas' slim straight stature but instead of the saint's kindly face this is a doleful-looking Santa who seems to have lost his last friend, and instead of Saint Nicholas' dignified robes this Santa wears an ermine-trimmed coat and long tights that give him the appearance of a jester in the court of King Charles.

From HALLMARK'S Historical Collection

fore Christmas." You'll remember that the poem describes Santa thus:

tall and consistently thin until the 1860's when the famous cartoonist, Thomas Nast, began drawing the old fellow on magazine covers and as illustrations for books.

Nast's conception of Santa more closely resembled Moore's word pictures, but was still a long way from today's version. His idea, shown in many old wood cuts, was a short, pixie-like figure, round and jolly looking, but obviously incapable of hoisting to his little shoulders the enormous bag of toys he is generally pictured with today.

Children everywhere, however, owe Thomas Nast a debt of gratitude they can never repay. He not only popularized the figure of Santa himself, but also many of the pleasant and exciting practices with which he is associated at Christmas time. He pictured Santa building toys in his North Pole workshop, driving his reindeer, and receiving and answering children's letters. Nast is also thought to have originated Santa's red coat, the result of a cartoon during the Civil War in which he arrayed Santa patriotically in a red, white, and blue outfit.

Artists have depicted Santa in almost every conceivable characterization. He has been painted as a tiny, elfin creature in a frock-tail coat with pointed collar, a belled cap and long, pointed shoes. He has been tall and thin, short and rolypoly, gaunt and ragged. His beard has been long or short, full or scraggly, and trimmed in a variety of fashions.

It was not until the 1900's that Santa began generally to take on the girth and stature of the beloved figure we know today, graphically illustrated in recent years by the plump, genial, indulgent old fellow conceived by artist Norman Rockwell. But even though the painted pictures have been very different, his characteristics have remained the

● An early version of Santa on Christmas cards pictured him as a tiny elfin creature whose only resemblance to today's version was a flowing white beard.
Hallmark's Historical Collection

● HALLMARK'S HISTORICAL COLLECTION—Lower center: The original Saint Nicholas,. bishop of Myra, a tall, stately man who resembled very little our present-day Santa Claus. At left is the version of the early Dutch in America.

same. He was always good and kind, and he was a generous bearer of gifts.

The legend of Saint Nicholas, brought to America by early Dutch settlers, gradually merged with the Christmas customs of many other nationalities who immigrated here. The original thin Santa of those early days of this country was supposed to be a likeness of the original Saint Nicholas. He was a tall, straight-shouldered man with a kindly face, usually pictured in his bishop's robes. In some paintings Saint Nicholas was depicted with three children standing in a tub at his side. Why the tub no one seems to know.

He was the saint of children, scholars, sailors, and merchants. A legend of his secret bestowal of dowries upon the three daughters of a very poor man is one way of explaining the origin of the old custom of giving presents in secret on the Eve of Saint Nicholas, December 6th.

It seemed difficult for artists to break away from the original conception of Saint Nicholas. As late as 1881 they were still painting tall, thin Santas. Possibly this was because they thought that they had to make him thin enough to come down the chimney, a factor that worries youngsters even today.

But Santa has now become traditional. Probably no great changes will be made in either his stature or his dress in the years to come.

16

So Right...So Wrong

L. J. Huber

WHEN I was younger, I considered myself quite a ball of fire. I might even have ignited the world and got scorched in the process had not my Aunt Kate kept me watered down.

Aunt Kate is the lady who steered me through many trials and tribulations after my mother died. In the vernacular of the day, she "raised" me. Dad, who was away most of the time as a salesman, provided the ways and means, but she produced the whys and wherefores.

In high school I had dates for the various social activities with a girl named Ellen Shields. She was a nice girl and, in my estimation, quite lucky to be escorted by me. It was hard for me to understand why she never gushed over her success.

Came fall and college. In the natural course of the calendar came the trip home for Christmas. The first matter that met my approval was the hockey game with our traditional rival high school. I put out the money for two tickets knowing that I, with my perfect personality, would have no trouble getting a companion. I contacted Ellen. She agreed that it would be a pretty nice way to spend an afternoon.

I dressed in my best sports outfit, which made me fair fodder for the fair ones. I walked to Ellen's house just to give the town a chance to see me and my finery.

"Ellen in?" I asked Mr. Shields when he answered my ring.

"No, Joe," the man looked surprised. "She's out somewhere."

"I had a date with her," I said.

"I'm sorry, Joe," he returned. "I haven't the least idea where she went. I'll tell her you were here."

"Thank you." I turned like a whirling dervish.

There is nothing flatter than a deflated youth, especially when he has been so very high before the pin is stuck into him. I gulped away my frustration, but it did not seem to help. Deep inside there was rising disdain for a certain young lady who had jilted and jolted me.

The new tie that had been flashed for the occasion seemed very dull. The hat, worn at a rakish angle, weighed heavily on my bowed head.

I slumped my way home, and dropped into a living room chair. The thud must have been very loud, because Aunt Kate looked up from her book.

"Game called off?" she asked.

"She stood me up," I snorted.

"Hmmmm," my aunt muttered. "Why?"

"I don't know," I roared. "She can't do this to me."

"She did it," she reminded. "What happened?"

That question opened the flood gates. I told my story and I embellished it with adjectives that emphasized the indignation within me.

17

No girl could get away with it. Making arrangements with me and then, in cold blood, forgetting them was a low blow to my pride.

"I'll give her a piece of my mind, Aunt Kate," I announced.

"Call her up?" she asked.

"No, I don't want to talk with her. But that won't stop me from telling her a thing or two. I'll drop her a note that will scorch the paint right off the mail box."

"You're being hasty, Joe," she tried to placate me. For a moment, I thought she was going to order me to use better sense. She didn't. As I went to the desk, she was letting me have enough rope for the hanging.

"Why not give her a chance to explain, Joe?" she started.

"There's nothing to explain, Aunt Kate. I had two tickets to the game and she ruined the day for me. It's —it's—it's," I stammered.

"Handalucial," she suggested.

"What does that mean?" I asked.

"Nothing. It's a word I made up to keep you from biting your tongue."

When the note was finished, I addressed it and stamped it. It was a dandy piece of denunciation. The words were short and to the point.

"I'll drop it in the mail box for you," Aunt Kate offered. "I'm going to the store."

"Thanks," I said.

She put on her hat and coat and left me to my own devices. Now that the matter had been lifted from my chest, it made me feel lighter. I was too miffed to go to the game alone. I nursed my disappointment by munching on an apple. I was about to start on my second one

18

when the phone rang. It was Ellen.

"Well?" I said coldly.

"I want to apologize and explain, Joe," she told me.

"Oh," I oozed. "Why?"

"I stopped at Kit Smith's place right after lunch, Joe," she talked as she ignored my sarcasm. "Her mother got deathly sick very suddenly. We called a doctor and rushed her to the hospital for an emergency operation. I couldn't get away long enough to call and explain. In fact, I'm calling from the hospital right now. I hope you'll forgive me, Joe."

My answer was muffled by the thought of the things that I had said in the note. They would be hard to explain. I would have given my last chance at the breakfast table to have it back.

"I'll call you later, Ellen," I finally managed to mumble.

I sat wondering what would happen if I ever did call her again. I could see that nasty note swimming in front of my eyes. Aunt Kate came in just then carrying a loaf of bread and some cold cuts.

"Where's the letter?" I jumped at her.

"In the mail box," she replied.

I groaned. I had had the fleeting hope that my aunt might have forgotten to mail the missile. Kate put down her packages. She asked what had happened and I told her.

"Why," she said, after letting me suffer a bit, "don't you ask me which mail box I used for your letter?"

"Not the one on the corner?" I jumped at this new lease of life.

"No," she said softly. "The one on the front porch. I reasoned that the mail man could pick it up there in the morning. That is, if you still want it sent."

Flowers

BETWEEN THE ROWS

L. R. LINTON

OUR town clock was striking ten. Outside the night was cold. The first snowflakes of the season were falling thick and fast, intent on their glamorizing job of hiding the city's dirt and grime.

In my office doing some monthly reports, I stretched and yawned. It had been a long day, and I was too tired to sort out the clutter on my desk. So with one swoop I pushed it into an empty drawer.

As the drawer banged shut I heard the soft turning of a knob. The door was on the far side of the large office. My desk light was the only one on, so I couldn't see who stepped in.

"Hello" . . . I said to the pool of darkness. I walked across to the counter and switched on a light. There stood the most abject specimen of humanity I had ever seen.

He was tall and terribly thin. His head was covered with frizzy black hair, and he was dressed in some ragged overalls and a torn shirt. Although the night was bitter, he wore no overcoat. His feet, covered with fast melting snow, were shod only in light slippers. Except for a gray line around the mouth, his face was black as coal.

"Well?" I barked. I hadn't meant to sound so sharp, so I added more quietly, "What can I do for you?"

The poor fellow was shaking so he could scarcely speak.

"I saw your light, sir, and I was cold." In spite of his misery the man had a kind of dignity. His voice was soft, and he spoke in a slurred sort of English.

I unlatched the counter gate.

"Come on in and warm up. When did you eat last?"

Instead of answering he moved to the large floor grate where the heat was pouring up. "It's the first time I've been warm for weeks." Then he added, "I'm off the S. S. Maria."

"Ah, yes, I remember. She was rammed in the harbor, and they had to tow her into drydock. But that was a month or two ago, wasn't it?"

"Just seven weeks today, sir. When they found it was going to be a big job they paid off the crew."

It turned out that Moses was the only South African in the crew. In that time no ships had been headed for Capetown.

"Have you any money left, Moses?"

His voice was very low, "No, sir, it's all gone now, sir."

"Why didn't you go to the Sea–

men's Institute? They help stranded seamen. That's their job."

"There's a lot of people, sir, who don't like Negroes. I didn't ask anything from no one until I came in here."

"When did you eat last, Moses?" He began to count on his fingers. "It wasn't yesterday, or the day before that."

I handed him an old sweater that I kept in the office as an extra. He folded himself into it. It went nearly twice around his thin frame.

Out into the snow we went and across the square where the pigeons huddled miserably under the eaves of the band concert stand. Dan's restaurant was a bright arc of light, as was Dan's genial Irish face. He was busily ladling up bowls of streaming clam chowder.

"Good night for reindeer, eh?"

As we slid in at the counter, Dan pushed Moses a bowl of the chowder. It wasn't any too soon, for Moses was beginning to slump. The smell of food had been almost too much for him.

"Feel better?" Moses carefully forked up the last crumbs of Dan's delectable apple pie. I marveled that his manners had never betrayed his hunger.

As he laid down his fork he grinned at me, a most disarming small-boy grin. "Thank you, sir. That was good."

I muttered something about I hoped he hadn't eaten too much after being without food for so long.

"If I did, sir, it would be the first time in my life that I ever ate too much. Mostly with South Africans like me, it's been the other way around."

20

There was no bitterness in the way he said it. It was just a simple statement of fact.

Well, I arranged with Dan to give Moses what food he needed, and with another friend who owned a hotel to provide him with a room. After work, I would often call at the hotel. Moses and I would go to Dan's together for our evening meal. He would tell me of his life in South Africa.

Before he got on the boats he, his wife, and four children lived in two rooms in Capetown. He made thirty-five shillings a week and paid six shillings a week for the two rooms. After deducting their necessary expenses, there was about $2.50 left to feed the six of them.

"And so we were always hungry," Moses thoughtfully stirred the sugar in his tea. Then his face brightened.

"But that was before I went on the boats," he added. "Now we have a four-roomed house all to ourselves. My wife has more money to buy food, and I have a garden, too. Enough space to grow ten short rows of vegetables. Between the rows my wife grows flowers."

Moses didn't know it, but in those sessions at Dan's he was handing out some lessons in basic living. To this day I never see a pansy without remembering a treasured garden plot and the flowers growing between the rows.

It was while I was out of town on a short business trip that the S. S. Maria unexpectedly sailed to South Africa. I never saw Moses again. When I went to pay Dan his food bill, I was astonished it was so little.

. . . continued on page 46

William Temple—
MAN OF GOD

DOUGLAS HUNT

THE CONFERENCE was drawing to its close. There had been long and learned speeches on a multitude of absorbing religious problems. Now the assembled delegates were awaiting a final message from the archbishop. Legs were comfortably crossed and chairs suitably adjusted. Every preparation was made to listen without undue interest or concern to what would doubtless be a lengthy summary of the work of the conference.

In the ensuing silence, William Temple stood up.

"Be ye doers of the word, and not hearers only," he said.

Then he sat down.

The incident is completely typical of the man and of his attitude to life. Above all, he was a doer of the word.

When he had taken up his residence in Lambeth Palace, after his appointment as Archbishop of Canterbury, a friend said to him, "Well, I see that the people of Lambeth have for the first time enjoyed the spectacle of the Archbishop running to catch a bus."

That, too, was typical of Temple. Though an aristocrat by birth and a scholar by training, he had no trace of self-importance or snobbery. If you had told him that it was not dignified for an archbishop to run for a bus, you would have been rewarded by that gale of tempestuous laughter which was the envy and the joy of all who knew him.

Oh, that laugh! It would burst from him like a crowd of children escaping from school. It would sweep everything before it. It was the laugh of a man of God.

Only really humble people can laugh like that. Perhaps it was his genuine humility, the humility of a man who measures himself against God's requirements, that made him beloved of the people.

Instances of it are innumerable. At the age of twenty-nine he was appointed headmaster of Repton. He surprised staff and boys alike by his first sermon. "Reptonians—pray for me!" he said. The memory of those words remained for years with many who heard them.

Noticing one hot Sunday that the attention of the students in the school chapel was wandering during his sermon, he startled them into immediate attention.

"Gentlemen, I don't know if there is a devil," he suddenly roared. He paused, as a slightly apprehensive congregation wondered which of

21

their particular minor deviltries he had discovered. "But if there is," he continued, "I am quite sure that God loves him."

There was something Godlike in William Temple's own love for all people. He laughed with those who laughed and wept with those who wept. In a period when there was acute suffering caused by widespread unemployment, he was both gravely worried and furiously angry. "I was hungry and you gave me no food," he shouted. For him, "feed my sheep," was to be interpreted literally.

His wide compassion for all men gave him a genius for reconciliation. Again and again, in both church and state, he was called upon to iron out the differences between apparent irreconcilables. He was able to inculcate in each side that respect for individuals, even those with whom one disagrees, which was such a marked and Christian characteristic of his own attitude.

He was happy. He rightly considered that for a Christian to go about looking unhappy was a denial of the Christian faith.

He was imperturbable. No one ever saw him ruffled or in a panic. These little upsets which disturb the equanimity of even the calmest of us never bothered William Temple nor roused his wrath.

NOBODY COULD EVER REMEMBER A hurtful word or a stinging reproach from him. One felt that it would be blasphemy for him to wound the feelings of anyone in whom dwelt, in St. Paul's words, "Christ within . . . the hope of Glory." A friend of his has said that the only time

people ever saw tears in his eyes was when he had heard someone make a wounding remark about another.

Young men liked him. They liked his boisterous laugh, his own boyishness, his evident respect for them as fellow men, his honest sincerity.

While still a young don at Oxford, he became president of the recently founded Workers' Educational Association. He gave it a vitally creative role in the life of the nation. First-class scholar though he was, it would never have entered the head of even the most Marxian mechanic that this hearty young man was trying to patronize him.

His first dynamic impact on the nation was felt when, in the first World War, he became the prime mover in the Life and Liberty Movement. The movement aroused a surprising response in the army. Temple went over to France to get into direct touch with the servicemen. From one headquarters, he wrote: "We roped in major-generals in shoals."

One of these tried to enlist a junior officer in the Life and Liberty Fellowship. "What's the pension, sir?" asked the young man.

"Eternal life, stupid," replied the general. The young man joined. •

In 1921, he was made Bishop of Manchester. This great industrial city was the last place, one would have thought, for a scholar. The people did not think so. They took him to their hearts as one of themselves. In his address when he was enthroned, they heard him say, "Pray for me, I ask you, not chiefly that I may be wise and strong. But pray for me chiefly that I may never let go of the unseen hand of the Lord

Jesus and may live in daily fellowship with him."

In the general strike, he did invaluable work in helping to reconcile both sides. He convinced organized labor that the church did not—as perhaps it had done in the past—embody the reactionary spirit of a privileged class. Employers and employees trusted Temple, not because he was an archbishop, but because he was a man of God.

When he was Archbishop of York, he conducted a mission to the universities. At Oxford, the Church of St. Mary's was jammed on the first night. As the congregation of young people was roaring out the hymn, "When I Survey the Wondrous Cross," Temple stopped the singing.

Very quietly, he said, "I want you to read over the words of the last verse before you sing it. If you mean them with all your hearts, sing them as loud as you can. If you don't mean them at all, keep silent. If you mean them even a little, and want to mean them more, sing them very softly."

After a short silence, two thousand young men and women whispered:

Were the whole realm of nature mine,
That were a present far too small;
Love so amazing, so divine,
Demands my soul, my life, my all.

He wrote a pamphlet on Christian marriage. Perhaps it could be summed up in his words: "The reason for not joking about sex is exactly the same as for not joking about Holy Communion. It is not that the subject is nasty, but that it is sacred."

To so deep a lover of humanity the World War II came as a heart-rending tragedy. While he truly sympathized with the sincere pacifist who could not fight, it was clear to him that to fight, though an evil, was by far the lesser of two evils.

It was in 1942 that he was installed as Archbishop of Canterbury and Primate of all England. Perhaps not for centuries has as fitting an occupant of this great office been found for a time of such great need. To us who knew his ministry, it was a tragedy almost past our comprehension that he should have been called away in little more than two years.

People on the buses he used to run to catch looked at one another with tears in their eyes as they said, "Ah, he was one of us."

Among the first of the many cables from all over the world came one from President Roosevelt to the King. In almost every message it was stressed that not just England but the whole world was made poorer by his death.

Temple would not have agreed. Whatever our Father decrees was for him the best. His faith will reverberate down the ages in the words he used a quarter of a century earlier:

"While we deliberate, He reigns; when we decide wisely, He reigns; when we decide foolishly, He reigns; when we ' serve him in humble loyalty, He reigns; when we serve him self-assertively, He reigns; when we rebel and seek to withhold our service, He reigns—the Alpha and Omega, which is, and which was, and which is to come, the Almighty."

23

"GO YE INTO ALL THE WORLD"

24

■ This is another in a series of interpretations of the five symbols developed by the United Christian Youth Movement to represent each of the five program areas of the Youth Fellowship. Mr. Eller is editor of *Horizons*.

INTO
ALL THE WORLD

by Vernard Eller

THE symbol speaks of Christian Outreach, that area of program and activity which goes beyond service in the local church and community. It reaches toward men around the world through home missions, foreign missions, relief and rehabilitation work, the ecumenical movement, and peace and world order.

The color is green. Green immediately suggests the plant world and nature. More particularly, green suggests springtime, the season when earth leafs out into fresh, clean growth. Spring is a symbol of the hope, new life, and rich blessing that mark the end of winter's poverty.

So Christian Outreach is painted in green. To many people, whose lives are set in the stark blacks and whites of winter's desolation, the reaching out of a Christian has come as a crocus in a snowbank, as the bud on a pussy willow. God's spring can rout the winter of man's sin when a Christian sees his brother and reaches out. The world is

greener, life more abundant, hope better founded, a harvest more assured, in those places where men have taken the Christian gospel of service and love.

The legend is "Go Ye Into All The World." This is quickly recognized as Mark's version of the Great Commission (16:15). But the command is Christ's. He says, "Go!"

He does not say, "If any of you Christians happen to have time on your hands, and are not at the moment occupied with weightier matters, then I might suggest that there are some other people in the world who would appreciate your help. Of course, if you find it inconvenient, just forget that I spoke." No, Christ says "Go!"

Where to go? "Into all the world." We go not just to the places with good rail and air connections, not just to the spots where we are assured of a friendly welcome, not just to the peoples who will make valuable allies in a world of conflict.

25

No, Christian Outreach, like spring itself, cannot stop with a spotty coverage. It's got to be bursting out *all over.*

As with the other symbols of the series, this one is given a vertical thrust by the white stripes of God's presence in the background. The breadth of a Christian's outreach is directly proportionate to the height of his uplook. "We love, because he first loved us" (1 John 4:19). We reach out, because God first reached down.

This symbol features an unclothed man. This is contradiction instead of indecency. What has such a man to give to others when he hasn't even enough to clothe himself? But the artist was after a deeper meaning.

Christ says, "Go!" But to whom does he say it? Obviously he says it to each of his followers. "Go ye!" means *me.* But if the man in the symbol sported a derby, I could say, "Go ye, doesn't mean me; I don't wear a derby."

Above the man hangs a compass. It is there to give him his direction, to keep him on his course. But crazy compass that it is, it has no needle and points equally in all directions. Yet that is precisely what the compass of Christian Outreach is intended to do. The course of the Christian is into all the world, never in only a specially-favored direction.

As the man goes into all the world he carries a scroll. On it is written the good news that "God was in Christ reconciling the world to himself" (II Corinthians 5:19). That is the message we hold as we reach out.

"But that is no scroll; it is quite plainly a stretcher."

All right, have it as you will. It changes the symbol not one whit. The gospel of our Christ is a versatile gospel. It can be transmitted as well through a stretcher as through a scroll. It reaches out as well through action as through words, as well through a kindly deed as a persuasive sermon.

Undoubtedly the instrument in question is both scroll and stretcher. The effective Christian is ready to bring into play whichever is most appropriate to the occasion.

"But a further anomaly mars the work. Notice that the figure is that of a man carrying a 'whichever' but the shadow is that of the cross."

Strange, but that is the way Christian Outreach works—and it isn't optical illusion. It makes no difference what the serving Christian is doing—whether the glorious duty of bearing the holy scroll of God's word or a more ignoble job at the handles of a stretcher. In each and every instance, the shadow that the needy one sees coming towards him is that of the Cross.

He does not find it hard to understand what the Christian means when he says, "It is no longer I who live, but Christ who lives in me; and the life I now live in the flesh I live by faith in the Son of God, who loved me and gave himself for me" (Galatians 2:20).

DID YOU KNOW THAT—

Charles Wesley, author of the Christmas hymn "Hark, the Herald Angels Sing," was born in the Christmas month, on December 18, 1707, and that he wrote over 6,500 other hymns?

World-Famous Shelter

By Franklin Winters

IT'S a dizzying, zigzag road that leads from the valley to the top of Great St. Bernard Pass in the Swiss Alps. In these days autos are used to make the 8,000-foot climb. But once upon a time the traveler's greatest thrill was to ride up in a "diligence" drawn by five big horses all decked with bells and fly-flickers.

Leaving the picturesque village of Chamonix, far down at the foot of the mighty Mont Blanc, the road ascends by a series of switchbacks. Within a few hours we pass from a region of summer heat to that of eternal ice and snow. Here, in an atmosphere of scudding mists and cold as piercing as Greenland's, we arrive at the impressive Hospice of St. Bernard, probably the world's most famous shelter-house.

Long centuries have passed since Bernard of Menthon launched his noble enterprise. It was in the year 962 A.D., that he founded a monastery and hospice at the highest point of the pass. Here he offered generous shelter to the hundreds of French and German pilgrims who each year toiled over the treacherous Alps.

The dogs that were enlisted to aid the monks became no less famous than the brothers themselves. They braved the most furious Alpine blizzards in their sentinel-duty. Often they came upon poor emigrant laborers who, exhausted from hunger and fatigue, had sunk down in the snow never expecting to rise.

After their rescue by the monks, these forlorn wayfarers were patiently nursed back to health in the spotlessly clean infirmary of the hospice. The brothers in charge never withheld anything needed, whether it was shelter, food, or clothing. This was their way of revering the founder of the hospice, whose memory they cherished so faithfully.

When Bernard first went among the people of the Alps, there was much ignorance and idolatry practiced. So tirelessly did he preach and minister to these poor folk that he won many converts. One of his last acts was stopping a war between two great noblemen.

Although Bernard was not formally canonized by the Roman Catholic Church until 1681, it is said that he was revered as a saint as early as the twelfth century. His kindness to Alpine travelers could never be forgotten. His most impressive monument is the huge shelter-house at the summit of the pass named in his honor.

Up in the cloud-swept pocket of the Alps, in the midst of roaring cataracts, green glaciers, and yawning ravines, the hospice stands secure among the towering peaks. It is one of the places most worth visiting in Switzerland.

Those who come there by the Valley of Death (so called because of its many tragedies) can pause at the little cabin on the dangerous brink of the pass and telephone ahead that they are on their way. After the monks receive such a message, if the travelers fail to appear in a specified time, a searching-party of dogs is sent out. More than once people have been found in the last stages of exhaustion and have been rescued from certain death.

When strangers arrive at the hospice, their first greeting comes from the dogs. Usually a dozen or more come baying forth from the door. These are no insignificant pooches, but huge, lordly fellows, as anybody who knows the St. Bernard breed can testify.

All wayfarers are treated alike. No questions are asked. It is understood that each is to receive dinner, a warm and comfortable bed, and breakfast the next morning. As a last precaution before leaving, every guest is supplied with full directions and the necessary aids for continuing the journey.

No matter where a person comes from, the hospice is certain to make a lasting impression. In the reception room the brothers will show you the big piano which King Edward VII gave to the monastery more than seventy-five years ago. A host of world-famous folk have passed a night under this roof, and gone away with a new understanding of the work the monks carry on.

The climate is such at this elevation that some of the brothers have to descend to the valley from time to time in order to keep in good health. Even the dogs suffer from

28

rheumatism. They can lose their lives, too, in the snow. In one furious blizzard five big fellows never came back. After a long record of rescue-work, the aged veterans are at last allowed to take perpetual comfort before the kitchen fire.

The world's gallery of lifesavers holds no more impressive picture than that of these dogs setting forth to aid some lost and exhausted wayfarer. Behind them follow the monks in their big fur coats, high rubber boots, helmets, and swan's-down gloves. They are accompanied by their assistants, bearing long ash poles, ice-axes, alpenstocks, spades, stimulants, and food. It's the army of mercy on the march, following in the footsteps of the founder of the hospice, Bernard himself!

When the first heavy snows invade the pass in September, posts twenty feet high are set along the trail. But these soon disappear under the drifts and other posts are fixed on top of them. The greatest danger comes from the furious winds. The snow is blown about with such force that return for the traveler often becomes impossible.

Sometimes the dogs go out all alone. When they find a man lost in the snow or fallen down a precipice, they return to the hospice. Then the monks come on a run, and the traveler is borne on stalwart shoulders to warmth and shelter.

For nearly a thousand years the famous shelter-house amid the clouds has been the scene of countless wanderers being rescued in the nick of time. Small wonder its name has gone forth to the four corners of the earth.

Jolly
Old
Saint Nicholas

By GLENN D. EVERETT

TURKEY has recently issued a postage stamp that pictures the home of Santa Claus. What? They put the North Pole on a stamp?

No, they put the real home of the man who actually was Santa Claus on this stamp. For Santa Claus, despite all the myths that have sprung up about him, actually did live 1600 years ago. He was a leader of the early Christian community in Asia Minor.

He was St. Nicholas, the bishop of Myra, capital of Lycia. Remains of the Christian settlement are to be seen in southern Turkey today. Among them is a very ancient house said by tradition to be the birthplace of the saintly bishop. The stamp not only pictures this house, but above it is engraved an outline of the only known portrait of St. Nicholas, the one embossed upon the sarcophagus which held his body.

Nicholas was born about 280 A.D. and had been bishop for many years at the time of his death on December 6, 352. He is said to have been born of wealthy parents, to a life that would have assured him comfort and ease. He embraced the new Christian faith, however, and spent his life in the service of the church of Jesus Christ. He suffered im-

prisonment at the hands of its enemies during the persecutions launched by the Roman Emperor, Diocletian. Later he was released under Constantine.

That's about all we know of him, for sure. Everything else is tradition. The earliest biography of his life was not written until the year 847, nearly 500 years after his death, by the Greek monk, St. Methodius. By that time it was hard to separate truth from fiction.

In any event, we can be sure that Nicholas was a revered leader among these courageous Christians of the Fourth Century. Otherwise they would not have called him "Saint" after he died, or built a great church over his tomb. He must have been a rich man who took literally the scriptural teaching that he should give his wealth to the poor, or he would not have left so many traditions behind as to his generosity.

We know that he was made patron saint of prisoners because of the courage and devotion to the Christian faith he showed during his years of imprisonment. We suspect that he must also have been a particular friend of the mariners who sailed their frail barks into the harbor of his city. He was made patron saint of sailors. Greek islanders, when bidding good-bye to fishermen as they take off for the Mediterranean Sea today, say in parting, "May St. Nicholas hold the tiller."

Most extraordinary of all is how Bishop Nicholas became the patron saint of children. Some say that he used to give gifts to the poor children of his town, dropping gold coins in front of their doors as he passed by at night. The townsfolk never knew the source of the gifts until Nicholas died. Then on his feast day, December 6, they annually commemorated his good deeds by continuing the practice in memory of him. It is easy to see how this might eventually have become associated with Christmas and the gifts of the Wise Men.

As centuries went by, the tradition of St. Nicholas, crusted with a good deal of medieval superstition, became very widespread in the Greek Orthodox church. From there it spread to Russia where St. Nicholas became the most revered of all the church fathers, with hundreds of churches named for him.

The cult of St. Nicholas was brought to Germany by the Emperor Otto II, who married Theophine, a Greek princess. In the year 1087 crusaders, alarmed by the occupation of Myra by the Mohammedan Turks, stole his body and brought it to the city of Bari, Italy, where it remains to this day. That brought the cult to Europe to stay by giving it a shrine.

In the Netherlands parents would give gifts of candy at Christmas time to children who had been good. They told the children that the gifts came from St. Nicholas. In the Dutch language his name was "Sint Niklaes." When Dutch Reformed settlers came to New York, their English neighbors called the mysterious Christmas visitor Santa Claus.

The poem, "The Night Before Christmas," written in 1822, gave us the picture of Santa Claus as a "right jolly old elf," who comes through the skies in a magical sleigh drawn by reindeer.

In our popular conception of Saint Nicholas today, we are about as far from the true story of the ancient bishop as our picture of Santa Claus is from the actual appearance of the Greek Christian leader of the year 352.

Santa Claus, the myth, is deeply rooted in our present tradition of Christmas, so much so that he is more the center of this Christian festival than is our Lord whose birth it commemorates. If we are going to have the spirit of Santa Claus dominating the Christmas season, we ought, at least, to look back through the centuries at the actual man who stands, vague and shadowy, behind the myth.

The gifts we give in the name of Santa Claus should be given in the name and spirit in which St. Nicholas gave his gifts sixteen hundred years ago. He gave away his wealth in the name of our Lord, who commanded Christians to help those less fortunate.

He never sought gratitude or praise from those whom he helped. He did it so unobtrusively that the astonished people did not realize who their benefactor was until he was gone. Then they venerated his memory and honored him by emulating his good example.

That is how St. Nicholas became Santa Claus—and how we, in our day, can again make Santa Claus become St. Nicholas.

Cheers at Midnight

IT is hard to tell what the cheers at midnight on New Year's Eve mean. For some, they possibly indicate joy that the old year is gone. They are a way of saying, "Good riddance." For most, they probably show again the fact that "hope springs eternal in the human breast." They are the welcome for a year from which much is expected. At any rate, they make a boisterous bridge between the end of one year and the start of another.

But what if there were no bridge, no new year—just the end of the old one? Startles us, doesn't it? We can talk so glibly about the end of the year because we are so completely sure that God has arranged for a new year to begin immediately. As Christians, we can face the end of life called "death," because we are made confident by God's promise of immortality. Our honest belief that the new holds promise of better things should make the passing of the old an occasion of joy and hope.

This fifty-fourth introductory column of mine brings us to the end of 1956 and the close of my work as Editor of THE LINK. But the ending is made unimportant by our confidence that it only serves to bring us to the beginning of a new day when another editor will accomplish much that I could never do. If the foundations have been properly laid—as I hope they have been—the magazine will go on to bigger and better things. This is really a time for cheers at midnight.

— Joe Dana

31

Christmas Service of Worship

Carl R. Key

CALL TO WORSHIP:
O magnify the Lord with me, and let us exalt his name together.
Behold, I bring you good tidings of great joy.
The people that walked in darkness have seen a great light;
they that dwell in the land of the shadow of death,
upon them hath the light shined. Behold, a
king shall reign in righteousness.
His name shall be called Wonderful Counsellor,
the mighty God, the everlasting Father, the
Prince of Peace.
O magnify the Lord with me, and let us exalt his name together.

INVOCATION:
O Almighty God, who by the birth of our Saviour, Jesus Christ, into the world didst give the true Light to dawn upon our darkness; graciously assist us that we, adoring the mystery of thy coming into our poor humanity, may in thy Light see light, to the glory of thy holy Name. Amen.

HYMN: .... "O Come, All Ye Faithful"

THE CHRISTMAS STORY IN SCRIPTURE: Luke 2:1-14; Matthew 2:1-2; 9-11.

HYMN: .... "Silent Night, Holy Night'

RESPONSIVE READING: . . "Christmas Beatitudes'
Leader: Blessed are they who find Christmas in the fragrant greens, th cheerful holly, and the soft flicker of candles.
Response: To them shall come bright memories of love and happiness.
Leader: Blessed are they who find Christmas in the Christmas star.
Response: Their lives may ever reflect its beauty and its light.
Leader: Blessed are they who find Christmas in the happy music o Christmas time.
Response: They shall have a song of joy ever singing in their hearts.
Leader: Blessed are they who find Christmas in the age-old story of a baby born in Bethlehem.

32

Response: To them a little child will always mean hope and promise to a troubled world.

Leader: Blessed are they who find Christmas in the joy of gifts sent lovingly to others.

Response: They shall share the gladness and joy of the Shepherds and Wise Men.

Leader: Blessed are they who find Christmas in the message of the Prince of Peace.

Response: They will ever strive to help Him bring Peace on earth, Good will to men.

—ESTELLA H. LANE

HYMN: .... "It Came Upon the Midnight Clear"

POEM:

When Jesus lived in Galilee
He never saw a Christmas tree.
He never saw the colored sheen
Of tiny lights in evergreen.
He never saw the wreath of holly,
The packages so gay and jolly.
He just went on from day to day
And loved and helped in his own way,
So long ago in Galilee,
When Jesus lived beside the sea.

I think he would have liked to know
That we would keep his birthday so.
With fun and jollity and cheer,
With lights a-shining soft and clear;
With friendly greetings across the miles,
With secrets and surprises gay,
And joyous carols all the day.
I think he would have liked to know
That we would keep his birthday so.

—FLORENCE M. TAYLOR

PRAYER:

Our Father, we thank Thee for Christmas with its reminders of the new love that came into the world with Jesus. Help us through the coming year to keep this Christmas love always in our hearts.

The Christmas lights will go out.

The Christmas trees will shed their needles.

The Christmas songs will be silent till another year.

The Christmas decorations will go into their boxes.

But, Our Father, we would not put the Christmas love away until another year.

Let us keep it burning warmly in our hearts every day. Make it the sort of love that will be big enough to include more than just our family and friends. Let our love be big enough to take in the people we have never seen who need our help. Let our love grow more and more like the love Jesus brought to the world on Christmas. Amen.

HYMN: .... "Joy to the World"

BENEDICTION:

The power of the Most High, the presence of the Lord Jesus, and the overshadowing of the Holy Spirit, give you peace, love, and everlasting joy. Amen.

33

Daily Rations

BY JAMES V. CLAYPOOL
Secy., Promotion of Bible Use, American Bible Society

THEME: The World to Christ We Bring

Bible Study for the week beginning December 2, 1956

Bethlehem—Fulfillment of Prophecy

GRAHAM G. LACY

SUGGESTED SCRIPTURE: Matthew 2; Luke 2:1-20

AIMS FOR THIS LESSON:

1. To understand Christmas in its Christian setting.
2. To glimpse the age-long preparation for the birth of Christ.
3. To get an idea of what prophecy is, and of what it is not.

■ Christmas has been called "a festival of joy about a Person." Though you may celebrate the season in a variety of ways, and though you find strange Yuletide customs as you travel in foreign lands, the unchanging heart of Christmas is the joy we feel over the coming of Christ into our world.

In the long history of the spread of Christianity over the world, many so-called "pagan" customs have been drawn into the celebration of Christmas. I see no harm in them. I welcome them gladly, as long as they are in keeping with the spirit of the One whose birthday we are celebrating. Christmas is "the season to be merry." Whatever makes for innocent merriment—Santa Claus, lighted trees, the Yule log, caroling, gift-giving—can help express the boundless joy of this holy time. Of course, carousing, commercialism, false stories, and being self-centered destroy the spirit of Christmas by flouting the spirit of Christ.

Because one of the Gospels describes the coming of Christ by saying, "The Word became flesh, and dwelt among us" (John 1:14), the church associates Christmas with what it calls "the Incarnation." This word, coming from the Latin phrase *in carne* ("in the flesh"), reminds us that the life of Christ expressed the mind (or "Word") of God in human flesh and blood—that is, in personal form.

At Bethlehem this life began. But it continued its course at Nazareth, in the wilderness, in Galilee, at Jerusalem, and beyond the grave. Christmas marks the beginning of the Incarnation, but it takes all the rest of the career of Jesus to express the incarnate life of God in the world.

The Bible indicates that the birth of Jesus in Bethlehem happened according to prophecy. Matthew writes that, when wise men from the East

Dr. Graham G. Lacy is minister of the Central Presbyterian Church in Washington, D.C. He served three years as a Navy chaplain in World War II.

35

came to Jerusalem asking, "Where is he who has been born king of the Jews? For we have seen his star in the east, and have come to worship him," King Herod was troubled and inquired of the chief priests and scribes where the Christ should be born. They answered, "In Bethlehem of Judea: for so it is written by the prophet: 'And you, O Bethlehem, in the land of Judah, are by no means least among the rulers of Judah; for from you shall come a ruler who will govern my people Israel.'" What does this mean? What prophet is being quoted?

The reference is to Micah 5:2, which is here paraphrased. The Old Testament verse looks forward to a new golden age. King David had been born in Bethlehem. Later generations looked back on his reign as the golden age of the nation. So the hope for a new golden age is expressed as the hope for a new David. The new ruler is expected to come, just as David did, from Bethlehem.

However, this verse is expressed in a way that seemed inappropriate to a human ruler. Micah predicts the coming of a ruler "whose origin is from of old, from ancient days." He may have meant that his coming was part of the eternal purpose of God to raise up a deliverer. But, whether or not he meant it so, the verse came to be thought of as "mes-

on the event, making for an interesting story? Or, on the other hand, is it a rigid prediction with power to tie the hands of God himself, so that Christ *had* to be born in Bethlehem and nowhere else? It is neither.

The prophet is one who speaks for God. If he is often correct in his prediction of future events, it is because he knows what God is like and what our world is like. He knows that, given a righteous God and a world like ours, certain consequences of our action can be confidently expected. But God speaks through inspired *persons,* not infallible *words.* Not all prophecies turned out to be accurate. Some prophets were called "false prophets." Not even all inspired prophecy turned out to be accurate in every detail. Much depended on the judgment of free persons as to what ancient prophecies were being fulfilled, or should be fulfilled.

In his ministry, Jesus fulfilled many prophecies, not because he *had* to, but because he *chose* to. Even so, the significance of this prophecy about the birth of a deliverer in Bethlehem lies, not in any mechanical series of causes and effects, but in the wonder and the insight of the earliest disciples. They recognized that Jesus was the Deliverer eternally intended by God. They

come sooner if anyone could have received him and understood him. But it took a long tradition—prophets, saints, martyrs, the history of a people interpreted in relation to the purpose of God—to prepare a group of persons who could recognize Jesus of Nazareth as the answer to all their highest hopes, and as the Word of God dwelling among them.

Questions for Discussion

1. What reason is given in Luke 2:1-7 why Jesus was born in Bethlehem?

2. What does this reason tell us about the kind of world into which Jesus was born? How does it resemble our own world?

Bible Study for the week beginning December 9, 1956

Nazareth—Influence of Home and Community

GRAHAM G. LACY

SUGGESTED SCRIPTURE: Luke 2:39-52

AIMS FOR THIS LESSON:

1. To attempt to picture the home life of Jesus.

2. To suggest the influence of home and community on the later life of Jesus.

3. To appreciate the importance of early training in the lives of people generally.

■ After the birth stories in Matthew and Luke, the Bible tells nothing about the early life of Jesus except for one incident recorded in Luke 2:39-52. These years in Nazareth have been called the "silent years."

Yet they surely were not blank years. Out of them the Master came prepared for his great public ministry.

Much can be inferred about the home life of Jesus from information gathered here and there in the Gospels and from general knowledge of the times and the town.

For instance, in Mark 6:3 we learn, from a question asked by bystanders, that Jesus had four brothers and at least two sisters. He was a carpenter and the son of a carpenter. Mary, his mother, was living. However, it is likely that Joseph died when Jesus was still at home. He is not mentioned after Luke's account of a journey when Jesus was twelve. As the eldest son, Jesus probably supported the large family by carrying on his father's trade until the next boy, James, was able to assume the burden. Then he would have been free to begin his public ministry.

We feel rather sure that the home was a modest one. Many of the vivid and poignant parables of Jesus reflect such a home. He pictures a household where, if a single coin is lost, a woman sweeps the whole

37

house anxiously to find it. He recalls that two sparrows, the food of the poor, could be bought for a farthing.

We know beyond doubt that religion was central in this home. Luke 2:20-24 shows us the parents offering the infant Jesus to God and performing all that was required "according to the law of Moses."

Jesus never attended any great university. Scoffers once asked where all his wisdom came from, remarking that he had "never studied." For the answer, we must look to his home and to the synagogue school, where every Jewish boy was taught the Scriptures. His happy, ideal boyhood is summed up in these words: "And the child grew and became strong, filled with wisdom; and the favor of God was upon him" (Luke 2:40).

Not every Jewish family made a pilgrimage to Jerusalem every year, but the family of Jesus did so. Says Luke: "Now his parents went to Jerusalem every year at the feast of the Passover." In connection with this devout custom we have that single incident that sheds such light on those "silent years" and on the attitude of Jesus toward his parents and his home. It is the journey to Jerusalem described in the scripture for this lesson.

Notice several things about this story of a lost boy. First there's the love of his parents. They missed him and searched three days, sorrowing, until they found him. Parental love is the first requirement for a happy home. It should be the unfailing heritage of every child.

Notice what Jesus was doing when his parents found him. He was in his Father's house and engaged in

38

his Father's business. The question Jesus asked his parents is full of interest. He said: "How is it that you sought me? Did you not know that I must be in my Father's house?"

A chaplain once said that you can tell a lot about a person by asking his buddies where they would look for him if he were lost. Where would they expect to find him off base on a Saturday night? Where would they look for him on Sunday morning? After the police and half the town had searched for a small boy in Kentucky, his parents finally found him in a movie seeing the same exciting show over and over again. If they had remembered his interests, they would have found him sooner.

Jesus was pursuing his own absorbing interest in the work of his heavenly Father. He was surprised that his parents should not have known where they might find him.

Notice that, though Jesus was a gifted child hearing the doctors of the law and asking them questions, so that "all that heard him were amazed at his understanding and his answers," he went with his parents to Nazareth "and was obedient to them." Another requirement for a happy home is a willing obedience. "Honor thy father and thy mother."

There came a time when Jesus, like any young man, left his boyhood home to do his work in the world. But his character had been formed in those early years when he "increased in wisdom and in stature, and in favor with God and man."

If the influence of home and community meant so much to our Lord and Master, we may be sure of its importance to us as well. The homes from which we come and the homes that we establish are cradles of character. When loving parents teach their children the love of God, winning their respect and implanting in them interests that continue and grow with the years, they are giving them the same sort of start in life that was given the Son of God.

Family life is sacred. Let us guard it well and throw about our children the love and security of a well-founded and unbroken home.

Questions for Discussion

1. What does Jesus teach about marriage? Look up Mark 10:1-9.

2. Could God have spoken to the world through Jesus if his parents had neglected to teach him the Scriptures and to build in him the spirit of reverence?

3. Just what is meant by "Jesus increased in wisdom and in stature, and in favor with God and man"? Is that a proper goal for a young man to set for himself?

Bible Study for the week beginning December 16, 1956

The Wilderness—The Test of Decision

GRAHAM G. LACY

SUGGESTED SCRIPTURE: Matthew 3:1 to 4:11

AIMS FOR THIS LESSON:

1. To indicate the meaning of the baptism and temptation of Jesus.

2. To see in his later ministry the effect of decisions made in the wilderness.

3. To ask whether firm decisions made in youth are dangerous or beneficial.

■ When Jesus was about thirty years old, he went down to the Jordan River to be baptized by John. Who was John, and what did this baptism mean?

John, the Baptizer, was making a tremendous impression on the people of his day. When he came out of the desert, dressed in camel's hair, with a fiery message of repentance, he reminded the Jews of their prophets of old. The age of great prophecy had come to an end some six centuries before. Many had forgotten the demands of Elijah, Amos, Isaiah, and Jeremiah. People were hardly expecting prophecy to break out in their day.

But here was a man who dressed like, acted like, and spoke like Elijah, the dramatic prophet of Mount Carmel. Indeed, many people said that this was Elijah returned from the dead. They claimed that the prediction of the last two verses of the last chapter of the last book of the Old Testament was being fulfilled. (See Malachi 4:5-6.)

39

The message of John was: "Repent, for the kingdom of heaven is at hand." He baptized in the wilderness and preached "a baptism of repentance for the forgiveness of sins." To understand what this meant, we need to remember that in John's day only Gentiles who were converted to Judaism received the rite of baptism. When John demanded that Jews also be baptized, it was as if he excommunicated the whole nation and warned them that they could inherit the favor and promises of God, not by right of birth, because they were descendants of Abraham, but only by repentance for sin and by righteous conduct.

Jesus welcomed this prophetic voice. He liked its rigorous demand for righteousness and its awareness of universal sin. (To see the rigor of Jesus himself, look again at his teaching in Matthew 5-7.)

Jesus went to be baptized by John. Now why did he do that? This baptism was a symbol, or sacrament, of repentance and cleansing. Of what did the Son of God need to repent? Those who knew him judged him sinless.

The answer lies, not in some puzzle of his personal life, but in his growing sense of vocation. He was struggling with the great and original idea that God's Messiah would have to take the lowly path of Isaiah's Suffering Servant (Isaiah 53). He

the close of his ministry Christ died on the Cross for the sin of mankind. Here at the beginning of his ministry Jesus comes as a Servant-Messiah to seek cleansing for the sin of us all.

The experience of baptism confirmed the surmise of his soul that God was anointing him for this dual vocation. This assurance came like a voice from heaven. No one else heard it. But Jesus found his destiny in the words that echoed within him: "Thou art my beloved Son, with thee I am well pleased."

John Wick Bowman says that this simple sentence combines the "coronation formula" of Psalm 2:7 (appropriate to the royal Messiah) with the "ordination formula" of Isaiah 42:1 (appropriate to the Servant). The first contains the words, "Thou art my Son"; and the second contains the words, ". . . in whom my soul delights."

From this wonderful experience Jesus went immediately into the wilderness to test himself and his understanding of this fearful and exalted role. Alone here for forty days he struggled, in advance, with temptations that would later threaten to turn him aside from his chosen path.

He rejected the temptation to use his great power for bodily gratification or merely economic welfare— "Man shall not live by bread alone, but by every word that proceeds

Later in his career these temptations presented themselves to Jesus again, but never with the same force because here he defeated them once and for all. Men sought to crown him king (John 6:14-15); but this meant compromise with certain evils. He turned away. After his arrest he firmly rejected the thought that he could call on God for special favors (Matthew 26:53-54), keeping to the end his Servant ideal.

The Master's example of firm decision, reached at the threshold of his work in the world, is vitally helpful to us in our tour of military duty and later civilian responsibilities. Who doesn't appreciate the technique of thinking first and leaping next? How often we make mistakes through haste or thoughtlessness. How often we fail by just drifting along, without ever thinking things through.

Our Lord harks back to this testing time when he tells his story about the folly of building a tower until one sits down and considers the cost. He must have thought of it when he spoke of the wisdom of going straight along the furrow of life when once you have set your hands to the plow handles.

Of course, any decision should be subject to change in the light of fuller truth. But unless we want to be reeds in the wind, thistledown at the mercy of a summer breeze, we should be thankful to God that he calls us from our wavering, uncertain moods into steady and certain commitment to him and his will for our lives.

Then when later temptations come along, as they did even in the life of Jesus, we shall be able to deal with them more easily because we have already thoroughly whipped them in a testing time that led to firm decision.

Questions for Discussion

1. If the Devil had been able to convince Jesus, what kind of person would Jesus have turned out to be? What kind of religion would he have founded?

2. If man doesn't live by bread (that is, material things) alone, why do we spend so much time grubbing for it? Do we have the notion that man doesn't live by it *alone,* but that it accounts for about 99% of life?

3. If Jesus' ministry had lasted forty years instead of three, would he have had to change these early decisions? Would he have found it necessary to compromise?

No horse gets anywhere until he is harnessed. No steam or gas ever drives anything until it is confined. No Niagara is ever turned into light and power until it is tunneled. No life ever grows great until it is focused, dedicated, disciplined.

—Harry Emerson Fosdick

Galilee—The Roving Rabbi

GRAHAM G. LACY

SUGGESTED SCRIPTURE: Matthew 5:1 to 7:29

AIMS FOR THIS LESSON:

1. To get an estimate of the place that the teaching of Jesus holds in the Christian religion.
2. To understand the relation of the prophetic and the priestly elements in our religion.

■ Some Christians who, like the Apostle Paul, came to their faith after a dramatic encounter with the Christ, talk as if the only really important part of his life were its end—the death and resurrection.

But it was the quality of the life that gave the death its saving power. When the Jews presented a sacrifice to God, it had to be perfect. They believed that God required a lamb or other animal "without blemish." So if the death of Christ was understood as a sacrifice for sin, one reason lay in the kind of person he was during his lifetime. What he did, what he was, and what he taught made the vital difference.

Paul rarely quoted Jesus' words. Once he wrote to the Corinthians: "I decided to know nothing among you except Jesus Christ and him cruci-

law of love. His hymn to love in I Corinthians 13 is practically a portrait of the Master.

There are some people who discount the teaching of Jesus for other reasons. Some say it was specifically fitted for his day, but is not relevant to ours. Others believe that Jesus was an impractical dreamer. Some say that he didn't give us rules but laid down principles. Out of this confusion, what shall be our estimate of the place of his teaching in the Christian religion?

Let us try to make answer by reference to the largest connected body of teaching in the Gospels. This is popularly called the Sermon on the Mount (Matthew 5-7). Here Jesus says (5:17): "Think not that I am come to abolish the law and the prophets, I have come not to abolish them, but to fulfil them." His teachings do fulfill the law in the sense that they *fill* it *full*. They bring out the law's full demands.

No one was ever more rigorous than Jesus in the demand for perfection. It has been said that the Serhis need of the gospel. No man can read these chapters without realizing that he, like all men, has broken the commandments of God.

Does this mean, then, that Jesus was an impractical dreamer who thought men could attain to an impossible ideal? Far from it! So conscious was he of the shortcomings of men, that he undertook to do for us what we could not do for ourselves. He took our place on the Cross that our hearts might be won to repentance and our sins be forgiven.

Does this mean, then, that by his sacrifice he erased his earlier interpretation of the moral law? By no means. The purpose of his ultimate sacrifice, which acted out his earlier summary of all the law in the law of love, was to enable us to keep the commandments from the heart because now we love God.

Forgiveness is ours by the free gift of God. But, as Paul makes clear in II Cor. 6:1-7, we are not to receive the gift of God in vain. We are to approve ourselves "as the ministers of God, in much patience, in afflictions, . . . in labors . . . by pureness, by knowledge, by longsuffering, by kindness, by the Holy Ghost, by love unfeigned, by the word of truth, by the power of God, by the armor of righteousness on the right hand and on the left." (KJV)

As for the notion that the teachings of Jesus were relevant for his day but not for ours, the answer is found in agreeing with the general proposition that he did not give specific rules for particular occasions. Rather, he laid down principles which need to be applied to changing life

situations. He interpreted all morality in terms of the intention of both God and man. For example, see how he dealt with marriage and divorce in Mark 10:1-9. He did not deal with what we call case law.

In his teaching, this roving rabbi taught "with authority, not as the scribes." This speaking with authority was characteristic of prophets. That is why many in his lifetime hailed Jesus as a prophet. In his death and exaltation he was recognized also as a priest. He is shown to be the unique priest who offers himself as the sacrificial victim.

It has been said that the prophet is one who speaks for God to the people, whereas the priest is one who speaks for the people to God. Jesus performed the functions of both.

Sometimes a religion, or a church, is characterized as either prophetic or ritualistic. It is prophetic when it speaks to the world for God. It will emphasize personal and social righteousness as the ancient Hebrew prophets did and as Jesus did in all his teaching. It is primarily ritualistic when it speaks to God for the world, emphasizing prayer, sacrament, and worship in all its forms.

The Christian religion, when it is true to itself, is both prophetic and ritualistic. The ritual may be very simple, and there will be no vain repetitions such as Jesus condemned. These became unnecessary when he gave himself, once for all, for the sins of the world. But the church, through its sacrifices of prayer and thanksgiving, will remember that the Galilean prophet, whose words cut like a two-edged sword, is at the same time our great high priest, for-

43

ever making intercession for us and all the world.

Questions for Discussion

1. What elements of your present life or character are reflections of some of the teachings of Jesus?

2. What is the distinction between rules and principles? Make up a list

of principles. How about a list of rules, too?

3. If Christ was both prophet and priest, should a Christian minister be both prophet and priest in his parish?

4. In most religions sacrifices have to be made over and over again. How do Christians figure that Christ's one sacrifice is sufficient for all time and all believers?

Bible Study for the week beginning December 30, 1956

Jerusalem—Triumph, Death, and Glory

GRAHAM G. LACY

SUGGESTED SCRIPTURE: Mark 10:32-45; Luke 24:13-36; Romans 8:31-39

AIMS FOR THIS LESSON:

1. To call to mind the final week of the life of Christ in this world.

2. To show what the power of belief in the Risen Lord does in the lives of his disciples.

■ This closing lesson centers around the events traditionally emphasized in the church from Palm Sunday through Holy Week, culminating at Easter. Reading the suggested scripture will help to bring these scenes to mind.

As some observer has said, the world may ignore Jesus, but it has never been able to forget him. The dramatic entry into Jerusalem, the cleansing of the temple, the trial, the crucifixion, and the resurrection all bring into the brief compass of a week the picture of one "whose birthday is celebrated around the

world and whose death day has set a gallows against every city skyline." Who is he? It is Jesus the Nazarene, Jesus the Messiah, Jesus Christ, Lord and God.

Many people in the time of Jesus had claimed to be the Messiah and had been proved false. When Jesus decided to enter Jerusalem, the capital city, as the Royal One, the King of kings, it was for good reasons. He wanted to proclaim his messiahship, not in some obscure town like Capernaum, but in the religious and political center of his beloved nation. In Jerusalem he would enter the temple. Here he would face the religious leaders. During the great feast season of the Passover, he would reach the attention of more people here than at any other time or place. He then "steadfastly set his

44

face to go to Jerusalem" in the certain and stubborn conviction that this was the time and place to say to all the world that he was the Messiah. This he had already disclosed to his intimate band of twelve followers.

The Negro spiritual "Were You There When They Crucified My Lord?" catches the import and spirit of the scene on Golgotha. Every force that caused the crucifixion is present today. Injustice, bigotry, vested interests, social and religious blind spots, and sanctified practices were expressed then. Certainly no one can say these sins are not with us in full force today.

It is a cynical attitude to say that these characteristics are so deeply ingrained in man that nothing can be done about them. If this is the final attitude toward the sin of man, then every church should shut up shop and go the way of the moneychanger.

The church at her best proclaims the good news of redemption from sin and release from these bonds. The state at her best permits this life-saving gospel to be proclaimed. The public can be stirred from its apathy to show a real concern over the importance of this message. Our only hope is to keep closer company with this radiant personality. When we see how he baffled the cynics of his day, we shall understand how his spirit today can enable his followers to overcome the world.

We see in these closing days of our Lord's life the powerful and often blind force of religious prejudice at work. Religious prejudice is the worst form of prejudice because it deals with the most powerful emotions of man. It is so easy for a man

to become so obsessed with his beliefs that any who differ with him are enemies of God and worthy of extermination.

Religious forces and leaders were in the forefront in the trial and death of Jesus. Only because they were under the political rule of another did they bother to bring their prisoner to the representative of Rome, Pontius Pilate. They knew that Pilate would not understand the claim of Jesus to be the Deliverer of the Jews. But they were sure that he would be greatly upset over Christ's claim to be the King of kings. They played upon the fears of a loyal governor.

The tendency of many of us is to blame either the religious people or Pilate for the death of Jesus. Perhaps the finger of blame should be turned toward us. When we realize how often religious people are aligned with the status quo and are blind to the need of change and reformation, we can see the re-enactment of the trial and crucifixion. We crucify our Lord afresh when we are indifferent to the call of Christ to serve our generation. We crucify him anew when we are racially intolerant or nationally arrogant.

Whatever realm Jesus would enter in life after death apparently did not bother the religious leaders. They wanted to make sure that this disturber of the peace was not on the Jerusalem streets after Friday afternoon. To them, Calvary was the end. To the early church, Calvary became the sign and symbol of the beginning.

However we seek to account for the belief in the resurrection, we must admit that something hap-

45

pened. Certainly something tremendous happened in the thinking and feeling of those discouraged men and women who were his disciples to empower them to stand upon their feet and live their belief in a Risen Lord. It is only when this heart-warming and mind-stirring experience is revived that the church today is vital and strong.

Read again the suggested scripture, Luke 24:13-36, and ask yourself, Would I be an alert Christian today if, after reading the teaching of Jesus, I stopped short of a belief in his present reign?

The birth stories, the parables, and the crucifixion are all part of his fascinating life and ministry. But if we do not believe that "he rose again from the dead," our faith in his teaching is vain.

From those unknown friends on the road to Emmaus, to Paul on the road to Damascus, to you on the road to Somewhere, it is the belief in the durability of the good, the resurrection of the Holy, the real presence of God in Christ, that can warm your heart and command your life—today and forever.

Questions for Discussion

1. What do we do with reformers like Jesus today?

2. What factors led to the refusal of the disciples to believe that Christ had somehow been spirited away in the night and to believe instead in the resurrection?

3. The four Gospels do not agree on the details of Easter morning, nor on the time and place of the appearances. How important is this to us?

4. If a belief in the Risen Lord meant as much to us today as it meant to the early disciples of Christ, what difference would it make in our lives? What would we change?

Flowers Between the Rows ... *continued from p. 20*

"I used to try to get him to eat more," Dan laughed as he gave me change, "but when he was alone, he was always careful not to order anything expensive."

It was nearly a year later when a thick envelope arrived postmarked, "Capetown." It contained a money order, a dried pansy carefully wrapped in paper, and a note with a childish scrawl:

"My Daddy does not write so I am writing this for him. He says this money order will help for all you spent on him, but money could never pay for all you did. He says, God bless you, and he will make a cross at the foot of the page."

And there it was, a big bold cross made by one of the finest Christian gentlemen I've ever been privileged to know.

Christmas Legends

THE folklore of the Christmas season is fascinating. Whether true or not, these innumerable tales form the traditions of the holiday season. Animals are prominently mentioned in many legends and customs.

One Christmas legend tells of the little gray lamb with a longing in its heart to be white. It wandered to the dwelling of the Holy Family, lingering at the door. The Christ Child, seeing the lamb, beckoned it in. He laid his hand on its head, and it became white as snow.

Norwegians, Swedes, and the Swiss make it a special point to be extremely friendly and hospitable on Christmas, both to domestic pets and to wild birds.

A persistent Christmas legend is that bees hum a carol in honor of the Christ Child. In England, holly is placed on the hive to wish the bees a Merry Christmas.

Spaniards are taught to treat cows kindly; they believe that cattle breathed upon the Christ Child to keep him warm. Tradition holds that cows and horses kneel in adoration at midnight each Christmas Eve. Among the residents of the German Alps it is believed that on Christmas Eve all animals can speak.

According to one legend, a fierce storm raged through the Harz Mountains one Christmas Eve. Massive trees were torn asunder; only the fir trees were able to stand up before the gale. The trees heard the cries of distressed canaries, and called to them: "Come into our branches. We will protect you." Now, when your canary sings his sweetest, you'll know he is joyful about Christmas Eve in the fir trees that protected the canaries against harm so many years ago.

In Worcestershire, it was at one time the custom to give a bough of mistletoe to the cow that first bore a calf after New Year's Day. This was believed to bring good luck to the whole dairy.

In Syria, the youngest camel that accompanied the Three Wise Men is called the camel of Jesus, and it is this camel that brings gifts to the children.

In Bohemia a horse is taken out into a river at Christmas and walked against the current. The rider tosses an apple into the stream. If it hits the horse, it will be stronger during the coming year.

AT EASE!

A blushing young woman handed the telegraph clerk a telegram containing only a name, address, and the word, "Yes." Wishing to be helpful, the clerk said, "You know, you can send 10 words for the same price."

"I know I can," replied the young woman, "but don't you think I'd look eager if I said it 10 times?"

An old crossroads merchant wrathfully wrote a debtor who had promised time and again to settle a long-delinquent account.

"You are just a mule-cared liar. If you don't settle up, I aim to clob-

"He thinks it's that way."

"I changed my mind."

ber you until there won't be nothing left but a pair of suspenders and a wart. I want my money and I want it now."

He signed his name with a flourish, re-read the letter with grim satisfaction. Then he added the post-script: "Please excuse the pencil."

A lawyer named Strange was asked by a friend what he would like to have inscribed on his tombstone. "Just put, 'Here lies an honest lawyer,'" he said.

"But," said the friend, "that doesn't tell who it is."

"Certainly it does," the lawyer argued. "Passers-by will say, 'That's Strange.'"

"You look worried," said a man to his friend.

"Worried!" exclaimed the friend. "I have so many worries that if anything drastic happened today, I wouldn't have time to worry about it for another two weeks."

CPSIA information can be obtained
at www.ICGtesting.com
Printed in the USA
BVHW040512281118
534009BV00079B/2549/P

9 781332 852086